Self-Driving Cars

Haydn Sonnad

Published in the United States of America by Cherry Lake Publishing
Ann Arbor, Michigan
www.cherrylakepublishing.com

Reading Adviser: Marla Conn, MS, Ed., Literacy specialist, Read-Ability, Inc.

Photo Credits: ©Zapp2Photo/Shutterstock.com, cover, 1; ©FranciscoSoberanis/Shutterstock.com, 5; ©KIM JIHYUN/ Shutterstock.com, 6; ©Jarhe Photography/Shutterstock.com, 7; ©Syda Productions/Shutterstock.com, 8; ©Gilles Lougassi/Shutterstock.com, 11; ©Yauhen_D/Shutterstock.com, 12; ©Flystock/Shutterstock.com, 13; ©Sundry Photography/Shutterstock.com, 17; ©Korbitr/Wikimedia/Public Domain, 18; ©MAD_Production/Shutterstock.com, 20; ©Akarat Phasura/Shutterstock.com, 23; ©Albert H. Teich/Shutterstock.com, 24; ©Scharfsinn/Shutterstock.com, 26

Graphic Element Credits: ©Ohn Mar/Shutterstock.com, back cover, multiple interior pages; ©Dmitrieva Katerina/ Shutterstock.com, back cover, multiple interior pages; ©advent/Shutterstock.com, back cover, front cover, multiple interior pages; ©Visual Generation/Shutterstock.com, multiple interior pages; ©anfisa focusova/Shutterstock.com, front cover, multiple interior pages; ©Babich Alexander/Shutterstock.com, back cover, front cover, multiple interior pages

Library of Congress Cataloging-in-Publication Data

Names: Sonnad, Haydn, author.
Title: Self-driving cars / by Haydn Sonnad.
Description: Ann Arbor : Cherry Lake Publishing, [2019] | Series: Disruptors in tech | Audience: Grades: 4 to 6. |
    Includes bibliographical references and index.
Identifiers: LCCN 2019005997 | ISBN 9781534147614 (hardcover) | ISBN 9781534150478 (pbk.) |
    ISBN 9781534149045 (pdf) | ISBN 9781534151901 (hosted ebook)
Subjects: LCSH: Autonomous vehicles—Juvenile literature. | Automobiles—Automatic control—Social aspects—
    Juvenile literature.
Classification: LCC TL152.8 .S44 2019 | DDC 629.222—dc23
LC record available at https://lccn.loc.gov/2019005997

Printed in the United States of America
Corporate Graphics

Haydn Sonnad is an automotive enthusiast interested in electric, connected, and increasingly autonomous vehicles. He is a co-founder of Tesloop, a software development and mobility company based in Los Angeles, California. The company owns 7 of the 10 highest mileage Teslas in the world!

Table of Contents

CHAPTER ONE

How the Automobile Shaped America

In 1908, Henry Ford started production of the Model T. Since then, owning a car has become a **pinnacle** for achieving "the American dream." Millions of households have purchased cars in pursuit of convenience, freedom, social well-being, and **prosperity**. Except during an **economic** slump, the number of cars sold has increased every year. In 2017, around 17.5 million new vehicles were sold to Americans. With an average selling price of around $35,000, this represents roughly $600 billion of economic activity.

One of the biggest improvements to cars is the types of metals used to make them. The metals are much stronger and can withstand more force. Many cars now have large "crumple zones" on the front and rear bumpers. These zones absorb the energy in a collision, making the car safer in an accident.

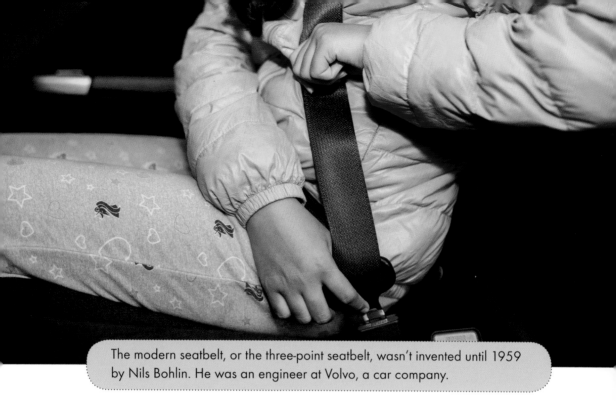

The modern seatbelt, or the three-point seatbelt, wasn't invented until 1959 by Nils Bohlin. He was an engineer at Volvo, a car company.

A Car's Influence

The car has influenced many parts of our lives—where we live, what we do for work, and what we do for fun. Before people had access to cars, it was hard to travel outside the city. Many people lived in **urban** areas where you could easily get around by walking or riding a horse or bicycle. Once cars became more available and more affordable, people were able to move away from the city. This migration formed the **suburbs** we know today.

We can also thank the car for much of the **technology** we rely on every day. Did you know that MP3 players, cell phones, and hard rubber were initially invented for cars? Today, practically everything in our society revolves around the automobile.

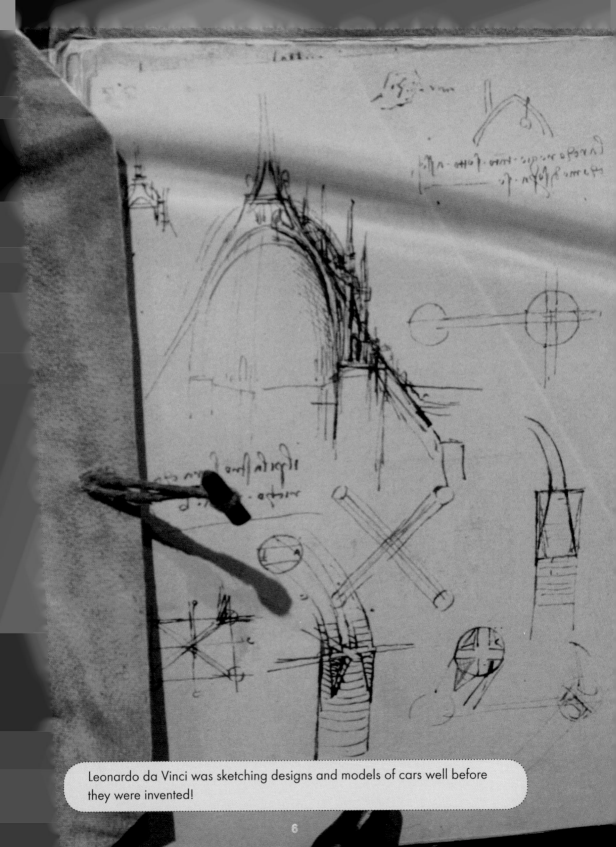

Leonardo da Vinci was sketching designs and models of cars well before they were invented!

Experts agree that unnecessary idling is not only bad for modern cars, but it's also bad for the environment and your wallet!

Drawbacks to the Invention

The car brought important advancements and improved the quality of life of many Americans. But it came with drawbacks. Every year, nearly 30 billion hours are wasted commuting to and from work. Over 30,000 people in the United States die in traffic accidents every year. And, according to scientists, almost 30 percent of all **carbon** pollution **emitted** into our atmosphere comes from the transportation sector, which includes the gas-guzzling car. Yet, there is good news. Cars are evolving, and soon these will be problems of the past.

According to the AAA Foundation for Traffic Safety, more than 58 percent of teen car accidents are caused by distracted driving.

Safety of Vehicles

Did you know that people weren't legally required to wear seat belts in many states until the 1990s? Or that airbags weren't required until 1998? While car companies were rapidly updating cars, basic safety features were still being discovered in the 20th century. Often times, new technology must be tested extensively before all the risks and dangers can be identified. For example, the general public wasn't aware that cigarettes were dangerous until 1964. But today, everyone knows that smoking is bad for your health and the health of those around you. Thankfully, cars have undergone massive safety improvements since the original models.

Many of these improvements are due to advancements in electronic technology. Cars today are equipped with all sorts of driver assistance features, like cruise control, parking sensors, and backup cameras. The mechanics of the cars are also smarter, enabling them to electronically adjust suspension, engine power, and traction.

CHAPTER TWO

The Electric, Connected, and Autonomous Vehicle

In 2007, Apple Inc. released a product that would reshape the relationship between people and their mobile devices—the iPhone. Today, almost 100 million people in the United States have an iPhone. But this did not happen by accident. The iPhone was designed to solve a few big problems that people had. Apple knew that to disrupt the mobile device space, it had to create a phone that combined five important features:

- User-friendly operating system
- Big screen
- Internet
- Camera
- Third-party application compatibility

Less than a decade after its release, the iPhone had changed the world.

Experts believe that by 2024, the driverless car industry could be worth $20 billion.

Today, we are seeing a similar trend emerging in the automotive space. Companies such as Tesla are taking a different approach to designing vehicles. In 2012, Tesla combined three key features into its Model S vehicle:

- Electric **drivetrain**
- Connectivity
- Autonomy

People have been designing electric vehicles (EVs) since the 1800s. However, interest declined once gasoline-powered cars became available. It wasn't until the 1960s that EVs were revived. However, they fell off the radar again until the mid-2010s. Now, EVs are here to stay.

Most car companies are rolling out cars with driverless features, like pedestrian detection.

Electric Drivetrain

Electric cars, also known as electric vehicles (EV), are much cheaper to operate than their gas counterparts. Electric drivetrains have fewer moving parts, so they require less maintenance and can last much longer. Additionally, it is cheaper to fuel a car with electricity than it is with gas. Electricity is also a more **sustainable** resource and less harmful to the planet than gas.

Connectivity

Connected cars are basically rolling computers. Connectivity allows developers to build applications that can be **downloaded** to the car, like web browsing, streaming services, or even connecting it to your phone. Just as applications, like Instagram, make your iPhone better, applications will make cars better. And like your phone, connected vehicles can be updated automatically, making the car better over time.

Tesla's Model 3 allows drivers to use their smartphones as car keys.

CHAPTER THREE

The Disruption

Ride-hailing services such as Uber and Lyft have gained widespread popularity. People have demonstrated that they are willing to make lifestyle changes when better transportation options become available. In fact, studies have shown that it's cheaper to use Uber than to own a car in cities like New York City, Chicago, Los Angeles, and Washington, D.C.! For instance, according to a study, owning a car in New York City costs about $218 a week, when you factor in monthly payments, insurance, parking charges, and gasoline. Taking an Uber short distances might cost as little as $10 per trip. Would you really spend $218 in a week in Uber trips?

Many heavy-duty industrial vehicles will most likely not be automated in the near future. These vehicles require special knowledge or skill to operate and perform unique tasks that are hard to be programmed on computers.

Waymo, Google's self-driving car, started an autonomous ride-hailing service in 2018.

Tesla is looking into releasing self-driving semi trucks.

Once cars can legally drive themselves, people everywhere will no longer need to own cars. Instead, they will be able to hail a driverless car to pick them up and drive them. This will have significant **implications** for the entire automotive industry.

Who Will Lead the Disruption?

At this point, it is unclear what types of companies will dominate the automotive space. Will it be technology companies, like Apple or Google? Will it be automakers, like Tesla or Mercedes-Benz? Or will it be companies that don't exist yet? One likely scenario is that companies and industries will collaborate with each other. This could create the best experience for users.

Who Does It Impact?

Already, we've seen electric, connected, and autonomous cars begin to disrupt the automotive space. In 2010, almost no automakers had plans for offering different types of electric vehicles. Over the following years, Tesla proved that many people were interested in high-quality EVs. Now, nearly every major automaker has plans to convert the majority of their cars to electric within the next decade.

This change has prompted the rise of other industries, such as EV charging stations. Companies like ChargePoint and EVgo have laid thousands of chargers around the world that any EV can use. Tesla, on the other hand, has been creating charging **infrastructure** that only works for its vehicles. Today, charging an EV can take over an hour, even with the best technology. But companies are working on finding a solution to this problem.

Many older cars are considered Level 0 vehicles because they don't have any automated assistance technologies.

Levels of Autonomy

The industry has created five standard levels of autonomy:

- Level 1: Driver assistance. The car may have features such as lane departure warnings and cruise control.

- Level 2: Partial automation. The car may be able to control the vehicle's speed and steering in optimal conditions, but the driver must always be attentive and ready to take over all controls.

- Level 3: Conditional autonomy. The car will be able to handle many aspects of driving, but not all. The driver must still be ready to take over the controls, but does not always have to be monitoring the environment.

- Level 4: High automation. The car can handle most aspects of driving, but there are certain situations that the driver must still handle.

- Level 5: Full automation. The car will be able to handle all aspects of driving at all times. A human may be able to operate the vehicle, but it is not required.

CHAPTER FOUR

The Future, Reimagined

Americans have spent decades driving cars now seen as outdated by the younger generation. Because of this shift in thinking, many industries will need to reimagine their strategies for the future. Here are some of the ways that self-driving cars will transform our world.

Commercial Drivers

Over 3 million people in the United States currently work as commercial drivers. These workers drive taxis, school buses, or large trucks that haul **freight**. Once cars and trucks can drive themselves, there won't be a need for these jobs.

Elon Musk plans to build an underground tunnel to be used only by self-driving cars.

City Infrastructure

Municipalities will need to add technology to everything that interacts with vehicles. Traffic lights, roads, parking meters, and other infrastructure elements will need to be connected. Another company owned by Elon Musk, called The Boring Company, is looking to solve the problems of roads. The company plans to build underground tunnel systems made especially for autonomous cars.

Driverless cars will also eliminate the need for many existing parking spaces and garages. These locations can be turned into parks or even housing units to better serve the community.

As of 2018, 29 states have laws about driverless cars. Pictured is Christopher Hart, then chairman of the National Transportation Safety Board, speaking about self-driving cars.

City Laws and Revenue

New regulations and laws will need to be passed. For example, autonomous vehicles may be restricted to low speeds when driving in urban areas. Municipalities will also need to think of ways to maintain the **revenue** that currently comes in through traffic and parking tickets.

Airlines

Flying short distances is often expensive, a hassle, and not much quicker than driving. Travelers have to park at and navigate airports, wait in long lines, and sometimes endure delays. Self-driving cars will make getting between cities much easier and cheaper. Travelers will be able to sit back, watch a movie or get work done, and arrive at their destination refreshed.

Auto Dealerships

Many self-driving cars will be part of fleets, rather than individually owned. Instead of going to a dealership and purchasing a car, consumers will be able to hail one using an app on their phone to take them where they need to go. Those who want to own a self-driving car could skip the dealership and go straight to the company itself. Tesla has already eliminated the middleman—in this case, dealerships—and instead is selling cars directly to customers.

Gas Stations and the Oil Industry

Since electric vehicles do not need gasoline, there will be no need for gas stations. This is a big deal. It's a positive thing for our environment, but not for the oil industry. Around half of all the oil produced is used for cars. Oil is a multi-trillion dollar industry, and it will be cut nearly in half. This will have major impacts on the economies of regions that are involved in the production and distribution of oil, like Saudi Arabia.

Oncoming car
Bicycler
Pedestrian

SELF DRIVING MODE
S1
30
30

The average American commute is around 30 minutes. If you didn't have to be the driver, what would you do with an extra 30 minutes in a day?

New Job Opportunities

Driverless cars will disrupt many industries and end many occupations. But driverless cars will also create new types of jobs. For example, cities will need to hire people to process all the data coming in from connected infrastructures. Yet, the new jobs may require a different set of skills. This may make it challenging for displaced workers to find new employment opportunities.

New technology can be scary and intimidating. This is true for electric, connected, and autonomous cars. However, the pros outweigh the cons. Embracing these technologies will save the lives of countless people, make it easier to get around, and reduce the amount of harmful emissions that enter our atmosphere.

5G Technology

5G technology will be a key ingredient in driverless cities. It will replace 4G as the next generation of wireless connectivity. 5G will allow for blazing-fast communication between connected devices. Cars will be able to communicate with each other and with the environment around them in practically real-time. This communication will help ensure an accident-free future! When dealing with cars moving at high speeds, it is very important to have reliable connectivity so that the cars don't crash.

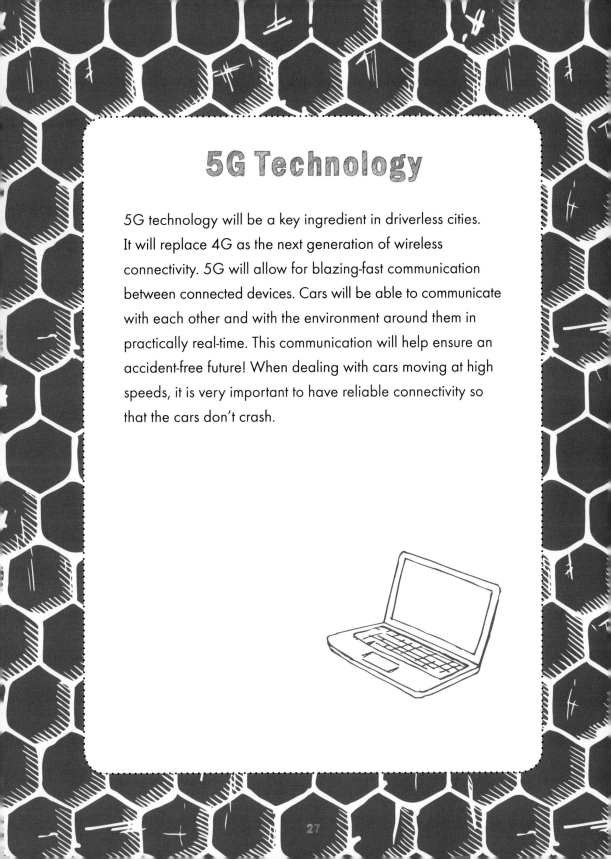

Timeline

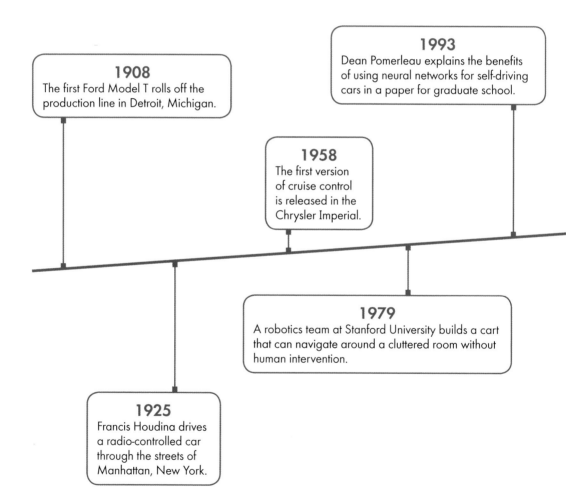

1908
The first Ford Model T rolls off the production line in Detroit, Michigan.

1993
Dean Pomerleau explains the benefits of using neural networks for self-driving cars in a paper for graduate school.

1958
The first version of cruise control is released in the Chrysler Imperial.

1979
A robotics team at Stanford University builds a cart that can navigate around a cluttered room without human intervention.

1925
Francis Houdina drives a radio-controlled car through the streets of Manhattan, New York.

2004

The Defense Advanced Research Projects Agency (DARPA) holds a contest for teams to race fully autonomous vehicles on 142 miles (228.5 kilometers) of desert. Despite the $1 million prize money, all competitors fail.

2014

The first model with Tesla's autopilot is rolled out in Model S vehicles.

1995

Mercedes-Benz and University of Munich researchers build VaMP, an autonomous car that can travel at freeway speeds for miles at a time without human intervention.

2009

Google launches the Waymo project.

Learn More

Books

Diaz, Julio. *Tesla Model S.* North Mankato, MN: Rourke Educational Media, 2017.

Gitlin, Martin. *Careers in Self-Driving Car Technology.* Ann Arbor, MI: Cherry Lake Publishing, 2019.

Newman, Lauren. *Self-Driving Cars.* Ann Arbor, MI: Cherry Lake Publishing, 2018.

Websites

Mocomi—Self-Driving Cars
https://mocomi.com/self-driving-cars
Discover more about self-driving cars.

YouTube—A First Drive
https://www.youtube.com/watch?v=CqSDWoAhvLU
Watch volunteers ride in Google's self-driving car.

Glossary

carbon (KAHR-buhn) also known as carbon dioxide, a chemical compound released into the atmosphere that can affect the climate

downloaded (DOUN-lohd-ed) transferred data from a computer to a smaller device

drivetrain (DRIVE-trayn) the parts of a car that generate power and transmit it to the wheels

economic (ee-kuh-NAH-mik) relating to the process or system by which goods and services are produced, sold, and bought

emitted (ih-MIT-id) sent out

fleets (FLEETS) groups of cars that are controlled or owned by a company

freight (FRAYT) goods or cargo carried by a ship, train, truck, or airplane

implications (im-plih-KAY-shuhnz) likely consequences of something

infrastructure (IN-fruh-struk-chur) the basic physical and organizational structures and facilities (buildings, roads, power supplies) needed to operate a society or business

municipalities (myoo-nis-uh-PAHL-ih-teez) cities or towns that have a local government and services

pinnacle (PIN-uh-kuhl) the most successful point; the culmination

prosperity (prah-SPER-ih-tee) the state of being successful usually by making money

revenue (REV-uh-noo) money that is made by or paid to a business or organization

software (SAWFT-wair) programs and related information used by a computer

suburbs (SUHB-urbz) smaller communities close to cities

sustainable (suh-STAY-nuh-buhl) able to be maintained at a certain rate or level

technology (tek-NAH-luh-jee) use of science to solve problems

urban (UR-buhn) city

Index